My W Book

by Jane Belk Moncure

illustrated by Linda Hohag

THE CHILD'S WORLD

ELGIN, ILLINOIS 60120

Library of Congress Cataloging in Publication Data

Moncure, Jane Belk.
  My "w" book.

  (My first steps to reading)
  Rev. ed. of: My w sound box. © 1977.
  Summary: Little w fills her box with a variety of
items that begin with the letter "w."
  1. Children's stories, American. [1. Alphabet]
I. Hohag, Linda. ill. II. Moncure, Jane Belk.   My
w sound box.   III. Title.   IV. Series: Moncure, Jane
Belk.   My first steps to reading.
PZ7.M739Myw   1984   [E]   84-17550
ISBN 0-89565-294-3

Distributed by Childrens Press, 1224 West Van Buren Street,
Chicago, Illinois 60607.

My "w" Book

(The "wh" sound is included in this book.)

Little  had a

She said, "I will fill my  box.

I will put my wildcat

and my wand into my box."

Little  put on her hat and cape.

"I will be a good witch," she said.

She found a

woodpecker

and wiggly worms.
She put them into
her box.

Little w found a weasel.

He wiggled into the box.

A wolf was after him.

Little  waved her wand.

"Wolf, be good," she said.
Guess where she put the wolf?

Little W found a well.

It was a wishing well. "I wish...

I wish I had something bigger for my things," said

Little W.

13

Little **w** found a

wheelbarrow.

Away
she went...

down the road
to the water.

"I will wade in the water,"
she said.

"Wow," said a walrus.
"What a wacky witch."

Little W said,

"You belong in my box,
walrus."

Little  put the walrus into the box.

The walrus winked at the wolf.

box

Little  went back to the water.

A whale was in
the water.

"You
are
so big," said Little .

Little found

a wagon,

a big, big wagon.

Away she went, right into a ...

wall.

What was behind
      the wall?

Watermelons.

"Let's have a
watermelon party,"

said Little W.

watermelons

wheelbarrow

wiggly
worms

26

wall

water

wishing well

whale

weasel

walrus

wolf

wagon

wildcat

And they did.

More words with Little

woman

window

web

watch

wallet

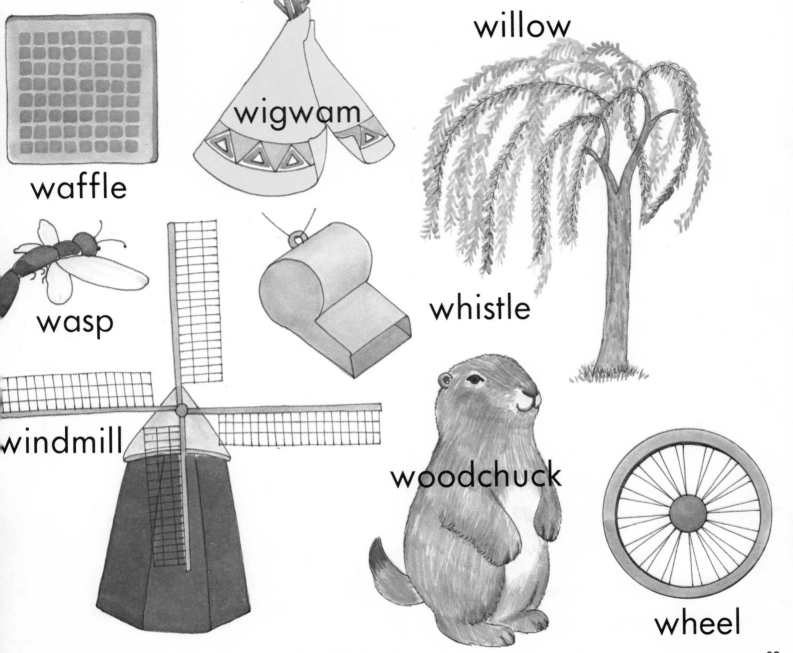

waffle

wigwam

willow

wasp

whistle

windmill

woodchuck

wheel

29